MY DAD
CAN DO ANYTHING

For my own dad, of course
—*S.K.*

To my dad, Robert, and my dad-in-law, Gary
—*M.W.*

By Stephen Krensky • Illustrated by Mike Wohnoutka

A Random House PICTUREBACK® Book

Random House 🏠 New York

Text copyright © 2004 by Stephen Krensky. Illustrations copyright © 2004 by Mike Wohnoutka. All rights reserved under International and Pan-American Copyright Conventions. Published in the United States by Random House Children's Books, a division of Random House, Inc., New York, and simultaneously in Canada by Random House of Canada Limited, Toronto.
www.randomhouse.com/kids
Library of Congress Cataloging-in-Publication Data: Krensky, Stephen.
My dad can do anything / by Stephen Krensky ; illustrated by Mike Wohnoutka. — 1st ed.
p. cm. — (Pictureback book)
SUMMARY: Takes a look at some of the many "special" talents that fathers have.
ISBN 0-375-82627-0
[1. Fathers—Fiction.] 1. Wohnoutka, Mike, ill. II. Title. III. Series: Random House pictureback.
PZ7.K883Mx 2004 [E]—dc21 2003002680

Printed in the United States of America First Edition 10 9 8 7 6 5 4 3 2 1

PICTUREBACK, RANDOM HOUSE and colophon, and PLEASE READ TO ME and colophon are registered trademarks of Random House, Inc.

My dad can do anything.
No challenge is too great.

He can put his head in a lion's mouth . . .

. . . or hunt for buried treasure.

On hot afternoons, he cuts his way
through the densest jungle.

My dad is good at sports.

And he is very artistic.

My dad can take charge in an emergency . . .

. . . and put out fires in a minute.

When we go on vacation, my dad is
an experienced traveler.

He makes friends easily . . .

. . . and catches criminals in the act.

He's not afraid of giants . . .

. . . or fire-breathing dragons . . .

. . . or aliens from outer space.

On very dark nights, he even scares away the monsters under my bed.

Yes, my dad can do anything.
He climbs the highest mountain.

He dives to the bottom of the sea.
But the thing that he does best of all . . .

. . . is spending time with me.